Hanzo Yang
IG & Twitter: @hanzoyang
Tiktok: @hanzoyangofficial

DARK AFFECTION
By Hanzo Yang

Jay, an American 23-year-old young man standing at 5 feet 9 inches tall with great physical strength, brown hair and blue eyes. He is cute and handsome. His life is on a winning streak as a well-known streamer and content creator with a remarkable following of over four million subscribers, earning him a reputation that's not just good, but highly respected among his peers. Jay is coming up close to his five million subscribers. On this evening in late spring, Jay is in his element, live-streaming to his eager audience. After two hours of live streaming, Jay usually reserved his last hour to connect with his fans directly by engaging with their messages in the live chat.

One such message, accompanied by a generous $20 donation, caught Jay's attention.

It read, "Loving the stream. What video are you currently working on for your channel? Can you give us a preview?"

With a smile, Jay replied to the highlighted message, "Well, it's another giveaway video because I really enjoy helping people, and I've been doing it a lot lately. I understand that some of you might be tired of it, but I'm passionate about making a positive impact. It is gonna be a bit different, but I won't spoil it for you."

As the stream continued, another generous fan, who had donated $50, asked, "Hey Jay, loving the stream. How's life going for you? Do you have a gf? If not when? And do you have any advice for approaching girls?"

Jay replied, "Hey there, thanks for the donation! Life's going good, and no I don't have a girl yet, and I don't know when but maybe soon and more on it later and as for advice on approaching women, I'll do my best to keep it simple. Really just take your time getting to know them and try not to come on too strong. A lot of women aren't always who they appear to be. Through my personal experiences, I've come across many women who were only interested in me for money and clout or as a streamer, not the real me. So, take it slow. Talking about getting women, I've got a date later this evening with someone I met on a dating app earlier today. I'm so hyped to see her. She's this fine ass girl that looks like someone I met back from my high school days. Anyways thanks to everyone who tuned in I'm out."

He ends his stream and turns off his pc.

Jay gracefully left his gaming chair and headed to the bathroom for a quick shower to freshen up. Late evening approached, and Jay was ready to meet the woman he had connected with earlier on a dating app. He wore a stylish black jersey paired with light blue jeans, a knife mounted on the back of his jean's hip, and his well-groomed brown hair showcased a refined gentleman's haircut. Completing his ensemble were $100 white sneakers and a luxurious $10,000 watch.

Ready to go, he sends a text message to the woman he met on the dating app. He got into his luxury car and set off for the restaurant where they will meet. He couldn't help but ponder the complexities of modern dating. However, he remained hopeful and open to the possibility of a meaningful connection. Jay drove for about 20 minutes to reach his destination.

As he arrived outside the restaurant, he recalled the hotel next to it, where he used to work. They were situated about 50 feet apart. The woman had chosen this spot for their first-time meeting, a date in a restaurant renowned for its Italian cuisine. It wasn't cheap, but it wasn't overpriced either. Jay parked his luxury car and stepped out.

Upon entering the restaurant, Jay scanned the area to find her. He spotted her at the middle table near the window. She looked stunning and voluptuous, even more so than in her pictures. His date, Don, her hair is blonde, she wears a fitted white short-sleeved shirt that has a v neck, paired with blue jeans, and a luxury watch. Accompanied by a pair of white sneakers to complete her outfit.

As they locked eyes, he approached her and greeted her, saying, "Don? Hey! How are you?"

She responded with a greeting, "Hey!" However, Jay sensed something was off about her energy. It seemed as if she might be forcing herself, not really in the mood to be there.

"Is everything alright? You seem a bit down," Jay asked as he took a seat.

Don responded with a mix of nervousness and excitement, "Oh, it's nothing. I'm fine. It's just that it's been a while since I've been on a date. But... how about you?"

Jay replied, "I'm doing well. Is this your first time here?"

Don nodded, saying, "Yeah."

Jay continued, "So, tell me a bit about yourself and what you do for a living. I'm just curious because I want to get to know you better, and your dating app profile didn't mention your occupation."

Don smiled, her tone calm as she explained, "Well, I'm currently unemployed and just collecting some unemployment benefits. But I did have a recent job interview, so we'll see how that turns out."

Jay responded with a smile, "Alright, cool."

A waitress approached their table and asked if they were ready to order. Jay and Don both perused the menu and ended up choosing the same dish - the ultimate cheesy pasta with chicken.

The waitress took their order and left.

Jay tells Don, "Hey, I usually do pay for a woman when going on a date with one, but due to my past experiences with most women that I go on dates with, they usually end up ghosting me or talking to some other guy while hanging out with me. So, I just want to let you know that I'm not going to pay for you if you're just another one of those women that's wasting my time. So, with that being said, you pay for yourself, and I'll pay for myself. And if things work out between us and we continue to see each other, I'll make it official, and I'll pay for our date next time, and so on."

Don looks at Jay as if she doesn't really care but at the same time seems a bit sad and nervous. She replies, "Yeah no worries I'd do the same too if I was in your shoes."

"Thanks for understanding." Jay replies.

After a few minutes their order came, and they ate as they exchanged a bit of words on getting to know one another on the surface but Don wasn't making much effort. Don, however, didn't eat much. She barely touched her plate of food.

Don is a 23 years old beautiful, gorgeous German American girl, with blonde hair and striking blue eyes, with a great body figure. She isn't skinny but isn't fat either. She's a bit thick, curvy, and busty with large round firm breast. Her cup size a G. She stands at 5 feet and 9 inches tall with a fat ass that's enormous. Her body is bigger than Jay's. She is currently unemployed and collecting benefits. Jay is falling for her but remains calm.

After a bit of eating and getting to know one another, they finished and paid. Jay left a $100 tip on their table. As they were heading out Jay purposely slowed his walk to stand behind her getting a chance to check her body out from her back. His eyes are locked on her curves and that big butt of hers. They stood next to each other side by side as they got out of the restaurant. Don seems a bit tense.

"Hey Don. So do you wanna see each other again? or hangout again?" Jay asked Don.

She turns to the right to look at him, but she seems a bit uneasy and nervous.

Don answers him, "Yeah."

Jay seems a bit happy but notices that she doesn't seem like she even cares about anything.

He asked her, "You sure about that? Are you okay? You seem a bit uneasy, and you barely touched your food?"

Don explains with a broken smile, "Yeah everything's fine. It's been a while that's all."

Jay smiles, "Hey I didn't wanna bring this up earlier when we talked inside because sometimes it is rude to bring up another woman for another woman to hear, or just bringing up comparison can be rude and unfair, but I just gotta say it. You look like this one gir-" Jay is immediately interrupted by Don.

"Hey! Do you wanna have sex?... If so, let's book a hotel right there now." as Don looks at him seriously.

Jay, surprised and answers quickly with a smile, "Ye-Yeah sure if you're fine with it." He didn't think twice at all.

"Okay. I'll call them now and book us a room." Don said.

Soon after booking a hotel room, she then tells Jay that she has to text her mom that she's gonna stay over at her friend's house. That way her mom won't worry about her.

"Hey, I'm gonna drive and park over there on the hotel side. I'll see you there, okay?" Jay said.

"Yeah, I'll do the same too." Don replies.

It's currently nighttime, and Jay and Don had just arrived at the hotel adjacent to the restaurant. While it wasn't a lavish or grand place, it seemed like a reasonable choice for a night's stay.

They stood at the entrance, ready to check-in. Jay broke the silence, saying, "I know you didn't ask, and you probably don't care, but I used to work here. I only lasted 20 days and that was like what, four years ago."

Don responded, "Okay, I guess that's cool."

After checking in, they made their way to Room 15 on the 2nd floor. Knowing that he will get to hookup with Don has got him really excited. Jay has a solid, hard on, erection just thinking about having sex with Don.

Don entered the room and immediately switched on the lights, then closed the blinds on the right side of the wall, next to the bathroom. The bathroom was directly in front of them, while the TV was on the left side of the wall. The bed was positioned on the right side near the window.

After settling in, they closed and locked the room's door. Jay, facing the bathroom, noticed that Don seemed somewhat uncomfortable as she turned to face him. Her body language and expression conveyed a sense of unease. There was a moment of silence between them, and Jay felt an uncomfortable tension in the air. He sensed that something was off with Don, and it had been bothering him throughout their time together. Frustration welled up inside him, and he couldn't hold it in any longer.

"Don!" Jay finally burst out, his voice edged with irritation. "Cut the bullshit! What's going on? You've been acting strange ever since we started hanging out. I can't take it anymore!"

Out of the dark from the bathroom that's behind Don, a man walks out quickly, standing next to her, holding a gun with his right hand, pointing directly at Jay's face. Jay is startled and confused with his two hands up immediately. He doesn't know what is really going on as he is in fear for his life. His heart starts to beat faster and faster as he is very still.

"Well done babe." Don's boyfriend whispered in her ear.

Jay asked, "What do you want?... and why are you doing this?"

"It's simple, we want your money, your card and pin number. Oh, and your car too, it's a nice car you have. Too bad it's not gonna be yours anymore." Implying that he's been watching Jay and Don the entire time.

Don is scared, frozen in fear as she breathes heavily as this was her plan all along with her boyfriend.

Her boyfriend then tells Don to go and search Jay while he stands and points the gun. "Grab everything, he's got on him." Don's boyfriend said. He then informs Jay, "And you don't try anything."

As she comes closer, standing right in between her boyfriend and Jay, she is then quickly grabbed by Jay as he ducks and holds her, using her as a meat shield, while he quickly pulls out a knife from his back, moving in forward, holding Donna, and stabbing her boyfriend right on the left side of his head, causing him to freeze with blooding spill out of his head.

Standing on his feet, Don's boyfriend tries to speak, but can't as Jay pulls out the knife from his head and goes in for another stab to his head. Don's boyfriend is now dead. Blood is gushing from his head. Don cried and screamed as it all happened so fast, she couldn't react fast enough to do anything.

She is trembling and falls quickly to only get back up leaning against the wall staring at Jay and her dead boyfriend. Tears ran down her face.

Jay quickly picks up the gun and points it at Don. He is in a rage breathing heavily in and out. He gives Don a mean ugly scary look with the intent to kill.

She is terrified for her life as she breathes so heavily and cries. "Pl-please, please, please don't! I didn't want to do this at all; he forced me to do it. I had no choice." as she cried out loud.

Jay screams and shout with rage, "Fuck you!!!, You fucking bitch! You fucking whore! You set me up! You and your boyfriend tried to rob me! And maybe kill me after, now I'm gonna fuck you up!"

His rage and anger terrorized Don.

Don cries with fear as she tries to speak, but can barely speak, "N-No we-we we were just going to rob you, an-and take off, that's it. And I didn't want anything to do with this, but he forced me too. I had no choice."

He shouts, "Fuck you! You do have a choice, you dumb bitch! You have the cops to help you, or family! And you didn't even bother to tell them?"

Jay then puts the gun and knife behind his jeans to be held as he then closes in on Don throwing a fist full of flurry blows to her head, face, and stomach. She tries to block using her arms, but fails miserably. Her arms took damaged too.

"I'm sorry! I'm sorry! Please!! I'm sorry!" Don shouts, but is punched and drops down on the floor and curls into a ball.

Jay grabs the top back of her hair, pulling it up to then back, and raising her as she sits on her bottom. He grabs his knife, pushing it up against her throat.

She begs even more, "Please don't. Please, I'm begging you. Please! I know you're a good and kind person so please let me go!"

Jay then starts bashing her in the face with the knife's endpoint handle as she is bleeding moderately and begs for him to stop.

She shouts, "Please stop! Pleeease! I'm pregnant! I'm pregnant, that's why we're trying to rob as many people as we can and run away."

Jay shouts at her, "Pregnant? You're pregnant? I don't give a shit! That is not my problem! You're just fucking lying trying to make me feel sorry for you!"

Jay puts his knife away again then punches and kicks her stomach constantly. Don is losing her breath, gasping for air.

She is in great physical pain, with a bit of blood on her, and covered in some bruises that's slowly showing.

Jay goes through her pockets and only finds her phone. He grabs her phone from her pocket and puts it in his pocket.

She speaks with a low breathy tone voice as she's trying to get some air. "Please... Please let me go. Don't call the cops on me. Y-You already done enough. Just let me go."

He then grabs on her right breast, as he brings out the knife again, pressing it up against her throat while she sits on the floor against the wall. He gazed at her body and eyes. His thoughts are dark, violent and sexual.

He wants revenge.

Jay starts to get a bit emotional, "you know... I liked you... I thought... I thought that maybe you're gonna be the one... or maybe I should just... rape you and kill you here!"

Jay lets go of her, then turns behind him and searches through Don's dead boyfriend. He found a wallet and opened it, showing the ID of Don's dead boyfriend.

The Description says "Name: Terry White, Gender: Male, Height: 5'10, Race: American, Hair: Brown, Eyes: Blue and State: California"

Jay then drops the wallet on Terry's face, who is nothing but a corpse.

Jay turns to Don, "Come on, let's go." he demanded.

It is getting late around 9pm. Jay grabs Don and helps her up. Don is weakened, but able to walk with Jay assisting her. Her ass is so fat, heavy, and wide, and her breasts so big Jay is liking the feel of her body next to his but at the same time is very disappointed in her. He is very on edge after everything has happened, he wished it could've been a better outcome.

She begs him to take her to the hospital, but he doesn't answer. They left the hotel without anyone noticing and didn't care about Terry's corpse as they made their way to the parking lot.

As they're in the parking lot, standing in front of Jay's car. He opens both doors on the left side. Jay puts Don in the driver's seat and tells her to drive, as he is in the back seat with a gun and knife in his possession.

Don sobs and asks Jay, "Where are we gonna go? Why didn't you call the cops on me or an ambulance?"

Jay, filled with vengeance, tells her, "Because I'm still trying to figure out what I want to do with you exactly. I'm not done with you yet, you must pay for what you have done to me. After all I do like you, but you just had to fuck me over and now I'm trying to think on what is best. Maybe I should just rape you and kill you, or rape you and then give you to the cops. Either way would be fun."

Don begs again, in a low, quiet voice, "please... just let me go already. You've done enough but don't turn me over to the cops. I don't want to spend my life in prison. I want to have this baby. I want to set better examples for me and my child."

Jay hits her with the truth about her pregnancy, "If what you're telling me is the truth, I already gave you a miscarriage. I punched and kicked the shit out of your stomach. You deserved it!"

Don weeps and sobs, knowing that is the likely outcome. There's nothing she can do.

In the car, Jay gave her a navigation for directions on where to go, as he plans on doing something to her somewhere. She drove in the night, as Jay was in the back seat just thinking of what his next move should be.

In his thoughts, "Should I just kidnap her completely and have her stay with me as my hostage? Should I rape her and let her go? Should I rape her and then kill her? This bitch honestly deserves it. Should I blackmail her and make her my sex slave? And if she refuses, I'll just give her up to the cops. Shit I don't know."

He lays back and takes a deep breath and exhales. He slowly tries to calm himself after being in a life-or-death situation.

Jay ponders and snaps out of it, as he now thinks carefully in his head, "Shit. What the hell is wrong with me? Did I take it too far? I threatened to rape her and kill her. I got so carried away with my anger that I forgot. I'm not a rapist, I should've never threatened her. I should've just called the cops. This isn't who I am, I love to help people and do good. And I want to do so much more but now here I am. I've never been in this situation before, not just that too, but I killed someone. Damn I thought I was gonna have sex with her, but she tricked me.

Everything happened so fast, I let my anger and vengeance take over. I should've known better because like I always tell myself a lot of people especially women towards me, they don't appear to be who they really are. I wasn't thinking straight. Even worse, this will be in the news sooner or later. My reputation will probably be affected."

Jay's thoughts continued, "Is this woman's name really Don? Who the hell is she? That's right, I got her phone. I should take a look at it."

As the drive continues, Jay pulls up Don's phone and unlocks it. She had no passcode on her phone. He goes through her text messages and reads the messages between Terry and Don.

As he looks through her phone, he sees her real name. It's spelled "Donna", and this name is slowly ringing a bell to Jay.

He slightly remembers this name of someone, especially with how attractive she is. Jay is slowly getting a small flashback but continues into her phone.

What he discovers is nothing but horrifying evidence of their robbery crimes and the verbal abuse towards Donna.

One of the texts says, "I will fucking kill you if you don't help me get this money from these people if you want me to be a good dad and start a family with you then you need to do as I say we need to be in on this together that is what family is all about "

another reads, "You better be ready when I pick you up if you're not then I will make your family pay"

Jay reads another text that's between Donna and her mom, its text, "Since you want to be with him so bad and you left with him when I said not too then that is it between us I disown you and you are not my daughter you're not welcome in this house anymore"

Jay continues to read more, gaining insight into Donna's past. He could sympathize with her, but he also feels bitterness and hatred toward her for what they had done to him.

As he delved deeper, he discovered that Donna had endured significant hardship, including blackmail and manipulation by Terry. Seeing the evidence of her bruised face in some of the photos left him eager to understand who Donna truly was.

He delved even further by going into her social media. There, he stumbled upon a picture of himself and

Donna was in a group of friends at the fair, but it was from years ago.

Her hair color and her style were a bit different. She was also a bit thinner in the picture.

As he examined the photo, he tried to piece together the memories associated with it, but he couldn't recall much. Confusion and mixed emotions washed over him as he looked at the image.

In his head, "Damn. What the fuck is this? Why does she have a picture that has me and her in it? This fair in the background, I don't really recall this, but she looks a bit familiar. Do I know her? Do we know each other?"

Minutes go by, and at a traffic light, Jay tells Donna to take a different route as she proceeds with it. Something is changing for Jay at this moment.

They arrived at their destination, and outside of what is in front of them is the fair that is soon to be open for summer, that's brightly lit up. It is beautiful and magnificent.

Jay hands over a water bottle to her that's been sitting in his car, she drinks up to quench her thirst. He told her to hand over his keys and exit the car and she did. Jay follows her out and tells her to sit at the head of the right side of his car. She sits in the front of his car on the right as Jay sits on the left side.

There's silence in the air, and Jay stares at her while she is looking down. She seems like she doesn't care about anything anymore. Her presence feels numb to Jay. She's fading away. She's lifeless. She's hopeless. She is dead on the inside. Jay sighs and continues to stare as he starts to feel a bit emotional. Something is slowly all coming together for him.

Donna let's out softly, "Why are we here?... Just get this over with... I don't care anymore... just kill me already if that's what you really want." As she slowly looked up to stare at the fair's rides that's brightly lit, a tear dropped on the left side of her face.

Jay says, "I went through your phone, and something just came up in my mind. What I saw... I'm not too sure, but it just made me think about this place and you and our younger days."

His face is frowning and filled with disappointment. He's remembering more of something.

"What happened to you?" Jay asked.

"What happened to you?... Do you know why I swiped for you in the first place?" he asked.

Jay explains furthermore, "It's because I liked you but... not just that too, you look like someone who I knew a long time ago, back in high school. Speaking of it right now, I think and feel like you are her. It's all coming together. You're Donna. The Donna that I knew back from high school, you were quite popular with how attractive you are. You were thinner back then and your butt wasn't this big. Your breast wasn't even this big." Jay is sad and laughs at bringing up the past.

He continues, "I remember I wanted to ask you out... because I really liked you, and I planned to do so... but a day later you just disappeared and never showed up to school anymore, and then something bad happened to me where I just kind of forgot about you. This fair in front of us was one of the times that we hung out for the first time. You even have a picture of it in your phone that I don't recall much of. Seeing that picture just made me feel like coming here. I don't know how to explain it."

As Jay brings up the past, it was like a knife through her heart. It's emotional for her, she recalls but can't really remember who Jay was. She misses the good old days too.

She lets out a laugh and cries trying to catch her breath. "I fucked up... I'm a fuck up... I was in love with this... fucking asshole and dropped out of school for him" as she cries and laugh more "you've met him... he's dead now... you killed him." she sighs and continues

"I don't know if I should be happy or sad... I don't know what to feel about it... or how to feel about it... I just don't care anymore. I'm guilty and I just want this night to end even if it means forever. I deserve to die." as she turns to look at Jay expressing herself.

As they brought up the past, they both sympathized with one another. Jay is emotional on the inside but isn't crying, his hatred towards her is slowly fading away as he knows that this is a woman who really needs help. She was controlled and manipulated. There's no peace and no balance in her.

He tells her, "Don't... I read your text... between you and your shitty dead ex... and your mom's too... I understand... and I can see that all you really needed was help. You're in a rough spot, where will you go? You don't have a place or a home to go to."

Donna cries, "It doesn't matter anymore. I don't care. I'm happy to die right now."

Jay stares down for a moment to think. He returns to his car and uses Donna's phone to call her mother. He told her it was an emergency, and that she needed to be hospitalized right away.

    Jay leaves the area but watches her from afar as she is just laying down on the ground crying in front of the fair.

    Minutes went by, and her mom came with the cops and an ambulance as she was taken to the hospital. Her mother may have meant it when she disowned her daughter, but with everything that's happened tonight, that changes everything.

    The next day, Donna wakes up in the hospital, where she is greeted by her mom sitting next to her.

"Mom?" Donna quietly said.

"How are you feeling?" her mom gently asked.

"Tired." she quietly spoke.

"Rest up, we'll speak later when you're better." Donna's mom said.

As she is awake an hour goes by, and Donna tries to rest up. A lot of feelings and emotions are running through her. She thought of last night, a night that was horrifying. She feels very sad, depressed, and guilty. She cries and weeps, sobbing in front of her mom.

They finally talked and went over last night. Donna took it slow and easy as she tried to explain everything.

"Tell me what happened last night? Explain everything to me." Donna's mom asked.

Donna takes a deep breath and explains, "Me and Terry... we we're trying to rob someone. It was Terry's idea. The plan was to pretend to hook up with someone on a dating app, so we could lure them into a trap and rob them when we got to the hotel. It didn't work out.

Everything went wrong and I should've never gone with it. I'm sorry mom."

Donna's mom asked, "Who was it? Who did you try to rob? And where's Terry?"

Donna cries as she explains, "It was a guy named Jay, I don't know too much about him, but I think he's kind of popular. And Terry... he's dead. Jay killed him and then he beat me up after. We deserved it."

Her mother, "Oh, thank God. Terry was never a good person. I'm glad you made it. If what you said is true then I'm very happy that he's gone, he deserved to die. He's ruined your life, our life."

"So where is Jay now? Why didn't he call the cops to arrest you at the scene?" Donna's mom asked.

Donna, "I'm not sure. I think we used to be with the same group of friends, but I can't recall anything right now. That may be why he didn't turn me over. I'm sorry mom, I should've never left with Terry all those years. I think I'm going to be locked up for sure."

Her mother tries to comfort her, "Don't worry I'm gonna get you a lawyer. Terry took your life away from you and me and I'm gonna do all I can to help you."

"Mom I..." as Donna tries to explain.

"What is it?" her mom asked.

"I was pregnant... twice. But I think I got a miscarriage. When I set Jay up, he was really angry and so he beat me up. He punched and kicked my stomach area. I'm sure it's dead... and gone now." Donna weeps.

Her mom is shocked, "I don't know what to say. I never knew you were pregnant. You barely told me anything after you left home. You said you were pregnant twice, what happened to the first one? Do you have a child that I don't know of?"

"No, mom, my first didn't make it either. I'll tell you about it another time." Donna explains.

Her mom replies, "Well, I think that's good! There's no way in Hell would I ever approve you having a child with a man like Terry. Imagine if you were to have a child with him, he wouldn't be able to support you or the child. He would just beat you up in front of the child or worse."

"Yeah, you're right mom." Donna agrees.

Donna apologizes, "I'm sorry that I never called you much, I'm sorry that I left, I'm sorry that when dad died, I didn't show up. I'm very sorry. I should've listened to you."

Her mom said, "I'm sorry too. I did all I could, but it wasn't enough. The cops wouldn't help me. I should've tried harder on my own."

"Everything will be better now." her mom comforts her.

They both cried and a small joy between them sparked. A mother is finally reunited with her daughter. It's been 5 years since Donna has been in and out of her mother's life. This reunion gave them a chance to rekindle.

Minutes went by and Donna's mom did some thinking.

She speaks to Donna, "Honey, I did some thinking, I know that what happened last night was terrible, but I would like you to thank Jay personally for bringing you back into my life."

"Mom, I don't know. I don't know him. He threatened to kill me and rape me, but I guess I would deserve it with how guilty I am." Donna explained.

Her mom calmly explains, "I believe he's a good person. A hero, a good man. What he did to you and Terry was out of anger but that was because you and Terry set him up. You angered him and let out a monster."
"I don't know mom." Donna said.
Her mom continues, "If Jay was a horrible person, he wouldn't have called me to get you. He didn't take you away, instead he brought you back to me. He did us a favor and we have to thank him for that."

"Maybe I guess." Donna slightly agrees.

Her mom continues, "You must thank him when you see him. As a mother, losing you was the most painful moment in my life. I didn't think I would ever see you again and I didn't just lose you, but your father too. Now you're all that I have left, I couldn't save you, but I think and feel like Jay did. So, we must thank him."

"I guess so. We'll see." Donna said.

Donna asked, "What will I do mom? I'm so guilty, and I feel like I should be punished for my crimes. I've hurted some people, I feel like I can't live with this guilt."

"Like I said, I'll get you a lawyer and see where it goes from there." as her mom comforts her.

"I don't think it matters because I know there's evidence out there of my crimes." Donna said.

"We'll see." her mom said.

The mother is finally caught up on the situation and she is well informed, she wants Donna to thank Jay for rescuing her, but Donna doesn't know if she can because a part of her fears Jay but at the same time felt like she deserved the beating that happened last night. At the same time, she also feels as if she's grateful to be able to escape a toxic relationship because she is now reunited with her mom. It's all too much for her to comprehend. It's mixed feelings everywhere.

The doctor enters the room to check on her and informs her of her miscarriage, as she already knew of the outcome way ahead. Her stomach and belly area are badly bruised.

She can barely move, as she is covered with a lot of bruises and minor cuts.

The cops came by later for some questioning and so on. Donna is scared and slowly answers the best she can. Her mother tells the cops to let her daughter rest and say no more, and not until she gets a lawyer. She is very tired.

Jay is at home, struggling to get any rest. Throughout the night, all he can think about is Donna.

In the morning, he gets up, takes a quick shower, and attempts to eat breakfast but finds it difficult. All he wants is to see Donna; he feels she deserves better.

After breakfast, Jay calls his mom to inform her about his experiences from last night. He explains that he will end up in the news and in court due to an incident involving a girl named Donna. Jay's mom is shocked by the news. They talked more, and she advised him to get a lawyer and suggested they meet up soon. They hung up.

He then goes and charges Donna's phone and calls up her mother. He explains his side of everything in a long story short. Jay is given the location of Donna's hospital stay. He showed up and made it to her room on the outside. He sees her mom and her. His heart is beating so fast as he stands there looking at Donna.

He's nervous but remains strong and calm as he enters the room. They looked at each other.

"Are you okay with me seeing you?" Jay asked Donna. "Yeah, I guess." she says in a low voice. Donna's mom leaves the room telling them she'll leave them two together.

"How are you feeling?" Jay asked.

"I don't know, I guess a bit better. And I don't know if I wanna see you." Donna said.

Jay sighs and apologizes, "Hey, I'm very sorry about everything, I could've almost killed you. I just wanna let you know that I only did it to protect myself... but... at the same time... I was very angry at how you set me up and so for that I wanted revenge."

Donna, "I would've done the same if I were in your shoes. I'm guilty of a lot of crimes, so I feel like I deserved it. I can't forgive myself for my poor decisions. Sometimes, things can go very wrong, and people die."

"Yeah, and hey I didn't tell you to the cops but I'm pretty sure they will find out soon." Jay said.

"Thanks, but it's alright. I already talked to them a bit and my mom told me to not say anymore until I get a lawyer. I guess I'll be going to court soon after I recover." she explains.

He asked her, "Are you able to afford one, though? If not, I'll get us one because I know I will have to testify, no matter what. I'm not sure how all this works."

Donna calmly explains, "Honestly, I don't know how it works too but my mom said she'll get me a lawyer and I don't think we'll be on the same side in court."

"Yeah, me too. Hey, how many crimes did you and your ex commit? What exactly did you two do? If you don't mind me asking." Jay asked Donna.

She sighs, "Honestly, I don't know. It's more than I can count but most of it was his doing. We robbed people at gunpoint and stole from jewelry shops and a bit more."

He sighs, "Well, here's your phone. I went through it quite a lot." as Jay hands it over.

"It's fine." Donna said.

"Aren't you afraid of me being here? Last night I threatened you." Jay asked.

She answers, "I don't know if I should be afraid of you or not. Or if I should be thanking you for getting me out of a toxic relationship. Last night I felt like I wanted to die so badly. So, if you did kill me last night maybe you would've done me a favor. But now that I saw my mom, I felt like there's a bit of peace, a small happiness. So much has happened and it's hard to process it all. My mom said I should be thanking you, but like I said I don't know because after all I'm a guilty person and I feel like I deserve to be punished. I must take accountability."

Jay sighs, "Damn I don't really know what to say. So, you and I go way back huh? Who took that picture of us and our friends in front of the fair? I remember the fair and our friends and you, but I never recall a picture of it."

"I'm not in the mood for this. I think you should go now, like I said, a lot is going on for me and it's too much to process. So, please leave me alone. All this is hurting my head." Donna exhaustingly said.

Jay sighed and exited her room to give her some space. He went outside for a while to get some air. An hour goes by, and Jay returns to Donna as he really wants to be by her side. He cares about her.

"Hey, I really want to be by your side and so I returned. I just wanna let you know that I'm not your enemy and that I really care about you. So please let me stay for a while." Jay begs.

Donna sighs, "What is it?"

"I don't know, I just care about you and wanna be by your side. Sometimes words aren't enough to explain it." Jay explains.

"I don't feel like talking to anyone." Donna explains.

Jay offers her, "Well can I at least pay for your medical bills? I know you don't have health insurance but I'm happy to help."

"You don't even know me. So just stop. And I'm just a criminal. I shouldn't have anything nice. So just go away!" Donna shouts, and turns her head away from Jay, as she quickly falls asleep.

Jay then sits down on the chair next to her. Two hours go by, and she soon wakes up and sees Jay next to her.

Jay sees her awake, "Hey."

Donna resting in bed silently and sadly stares at him.

She exhaustedly whispers, "Just leave me alone."

"Maybe for once in your life let someone help you. Aren't you tired of fighting all alone?" Jay kindly asked.

"I don't know." she quietly said.

A few minutes go by, and Donna momentarily thinks about the photo that Jay mentioned. She looks at her phone that's next to her and grabs it. She's curious and looks for the picture and stumbles across it.

It brings back a bit of memory to her, but she doesn't know who took it. She sees herself and Jay in the photo with some of their old friends back in high school during senior year.

"I'm assuming you're looking at the picture. Do you remember anything?" Jay asked.

Donna replies, "Honestly, I don't know. I don't remember much. It's been a long time since I even looked at my old pictures. I don't know who took it, but there's you and me there, and our friends from high school. I honestly didn't know that you and I met before, I don't remember you much but it's slowly coming together."

Jay replies, "You were thinner back then and you weren't this busty... and your butt wasn't as big as now. I'm not trying to say that you're fat or ugly. What I'm trying to say is that you looked a bit different and that's why I didn't recognize you sooner when we first met and honestly, I think you look better now, you look like a fine ass grown woman. I wouldn't want you any other way."

"Thanks, that's very nice of you. I don't think I've heard anything like that in a long time." she happily said but doesn't really know how to feel about it.

"So, when you're able to get out of here can you and I hang out sometimes? I really like you and I care about you. I wanna spend time with you and get to know you more. I know this is a lot to take in." Jay asked.

She sighs, "You need to leave. You're exhausting me with everything. It's just too much."

"I'm sorry." Jay sadly apologized.

Donna sighs and explains herself, "Honestly, I don't know if that's a good idea. Me and you, I don't know you like that, and like I said I'm guilty of the crimes I've committed, I've committed some crimes that's unforgivable... and I don't think I deserve anything good. I'm still gonna have to face a judge in the courtroom... and for sure I will be found guilty. I know where you're trying to get at and trust me, I'm not worth your time. You don't wanna be with a woman like me or someone who's gonna end up in jail or worse. I just don't deserve anything really. And as you know last night was the night that I got out of a shit relationship. I don't think I would be ready for any relationship soon whatsoever. It's very nice of you but I don't see it happening. I'm sorry, now leave."

Jay sighs, "I never said anything about being in a relationship with you. But the evidence on your phone and his phone. It proves that you were manipulated, and he was controlling you so-"

"It doesn't matter because I'm an adult and I took part in it with him, I will be found guilty for sure, and I shot a man in his arm and no I didn't kill him!" Donna shouted!

Jay sighs, "Damn."

They're both sad and heartbroken. Donna looks at Jay and sees his face frowning looking down on the floor.

Jay apologizes, "I'm really sorry, but I think you deserve better though. Anyways I'll leave you be for now, but hey let's at least call and text sometimes because after all you and I will be in court together so let's stay in touch. I still have your number. I'll call you, okay?"

"Yeah, I guess." Donna said.

Jay then walked out of her hospital room. He bumps into Donna's mother.

"We've never properly introduced ourselves, but I'm Dina." she explained.

Jay greets Dina, "Hey, I'm Jay."

Dina thanks him, "I just wanted to thank you for saving my daughter. For a very long time she was being abused and manipulated by Terry. So, I am very grateful that you have brought my daughter back into my life."

"Yeah, no worries." Jay said with a sad face.

Dina comforts Jay, "Don't feel guilty at all. Terry was a criminal who's committed heinous crimes that's unforgivable and he deserves to die. The cops didn't care to help me at all so I'm very happy that he's dead."

"Yeah." Jay said.

Dina asks, "Can I get your number to contact you?"

Jay, "Why? I beaten up your daughter a bit and threatened her last night. Why would you be so welcoming to me?" he confusingly asked.

She gracefully explains, "You did us a favor, you saved my daughter and I know you gave her a miscarriage but that's okay. There's no way in hell would I ever approve my daughter to have a child with a man like Terry. A person like that is not capable. Anything you did last night was out of self-defense and I know you wanted revenge. I would do the same too if I was in your position, I wish I was the one that killed Terry. I don't think you understand what it's like to be a mother that lost her daughter for years to only finally have her come back. So don't feel guilty of anything. I know you're a good person and I know exactly who you are."

"What? What do you mean?" Jay confusingly asked.

She explains, "You're a content creator and a streamer. Some people even consider you their hero. I've seen some of your charity acts that you did globally and locally. You were even on the news. Not just that too, but you used to go to the same high school as my daughter."

"Oh, okay. Here's my number. I gotta go." Jay said as Dina and him exchanged contacts.

"Wait!" Dina shouted.

"Yeah?" Jay stops.

She asks, "Before you go, I just want to know. Why didn't you call the cops on my daughter? Why didn't you turn her over?"

He explained, "Because I see that she was someone who really needed help... and that's what I do. I try helping people."

"Well, then... thank you." Dina gratefully said.

Dina is a 52-year-old woman who is a retired businesswoman. She lives collecting royalties, standing 5 feet and 8 inches tall. She is a very established successful woman.

Her eyes are blue, and her hair color is blonde mixed with a bit of gray hair strands.

Jay heads over back to his house, he cares about Donna deeply, he thinks about her constantly. He skipped live streaming for the day because he wasn't in the mood. He knows for sure that she will be found guilty, no matter what.

Jay's mother soon arrives at his house. His mother arrives as she is well dressed, wearing her business suit.

She is the CEO and founder of a popular beverage company named "Judy's Juice".

She is a wealthy and well-established woman. Judy is 50 years old, standing at 5 feet 7 inches tall. She has brown hair and blue eyes.

Jay's mother, Judy, hugs him tightly as they both see each other. She tries her best to comfort him, as she can see it all in his face. They both go over everything. As Jay explains, his mother doesn't agree with him about helping Donna. Judy is infuriated with what she is hearing.

Judy asks, "How are you holding up?"

Jay explains, "I'm a bit stressed out that's all. Mom, I know you will not agree with me on this, but I really want to help her."

Judy shouts, "Are you serious? She doesn't need help! That woman deserves to be in prison and locked up. If I am correct, I even saw them on the news a few days ago. They're criminals on the run!"

Jay defends Donna explaining, "Yeah but like I said she was being manipulated. She was blackmailed by her ex. This girl had it rough, give her a break."

She shouts, "No! It doesn't matter! And why didn't you call the cops on her in the first place? What the hell is wrong with you? You could've died and I can't bear the thought of that. We lost your father, and I can't lose you too!"

He sighs, "This is what I do mom. I help some people and try my best to help as many people as I can, you know that."

She shouts again, "You're so stupid! She's a grown woman! She could've gone to the cops for help, and she didn't. She chose this life of crime and misery. She must pay for her crimes! Donna is not right for you! I can see that you've fallen for her! I know that you love to help people, sometimes you just help too much, and too many people. Not everyone deserves to be helped! Like this girl, Donna! She doesn't deserve the help!"

He sighs, "Mom I-"

"Did you get yourself a lawyer yet?" Judy asked.

"No, not yet, but soon I will." he sadly said.

Judy, "Truth be told you can't help her. She will be found guilty, and she will be behind bars no matter what, even if you help her. Get yourself a lawyer right away. I'm gonna go now and I'll see you soon." After talking she walked out of his house.

Jay stares down silently, at a loss for words. His mother can tell that he has fallen for Donna, and she's concerned, wanting him to stay away from her.

Jay is aware of Donna's involvement in some criminal activity, yet he remains committed to helping her.

Jay's compassionate nature and big heart sometimes leave him conflicted about the best course of action.

He checks his phone to access the latest news online. On the news website, Jay comes across surveillance security camera footage that is being featured. The police have made a public statement about the murder, and on the news, they show Jay's and Donna's faces as possible suspects. The authorities mention that the crimes committed by Terry and Donna might be linked to Jay in some way.

Another statement being made by the police is that Terry and Donna have been on the run for over a week. The police are able to connect some of the crimes leading to Terry and Donna but furthermore is still being investigated.

Jay looks more into the news on the internet, and he can see that he is trending. He already knew that all this was gonna have an effect sooner or later.

Deciding to log into his social media accounts to make a brief statement, Jay soon discovered that the notifications on his phone were overwhelming, even though he had it muted. His posts and mentions were flooding in, creating an unprecedented trend and notification frenzy.

Feeling overwhelmed, he made the decision not to make any public statements until he had legal representation.

Jay was honestly at a loss for words and decided to put his phone away for the time being.

Jay, overwhelmed with stress, and minutes turn into hours as another day dawns. Sleep and rest elude him, leaving him fatigued and on edge. In the morning, he takes a shower but moves through the routine robotically. The warm, steamy water surrounds him, creating a moment of comfort amidst the chaos.

Jay turns to face the wall, closes his eyes, and drifts back to his high school days in reflection. As the water ran down onto his back it took him back to the time, where he officially hung out with Donna for the first time.

It was five years ago during the beginning of senior year when he and his friends went to the state fair before it closed. It was late summer, and school had barely started.

Jay and Donna met in high school and talked a bit here and there but never officially hung out until this moment at the state fair.

They all took the public transportation bus to get to the fair. In the bus Jay sat next to Donna.

"Hey! Donna." Jay smiled.

"Oh hey!" Donna smiles back.

"We've never officially hung out until now. So that's cool." Jay said.

"What? No, we hang out at school." Donna replied.

Jay, "Not really, we had like one class together and talked a few times that's it. But now that we're going to the fair it's gonna be cool."

"You smoke?" Donna asked.

"No. Do you smoke?" Jay asked Donna.

"Yeah, only weed though. You ever wanna try?" Donna says.

"No, I'm good." he declines.

Jay is a bit disappointed with what he's heard from Donna. He really likes her, and he is not a smoker himself and he doesn't do marijuana. All this is new news to him.

"If you ever change your mind, come find me and I'll hook you up with the best." she said.

"Does your parents know?" Jay asked.

"No." She replied.

"Besides weed, do you drink?" Jay continues to question her.

"Yeah sometimes. And you? You drink?" Donna asked.

"No, I don't drink at all." Jay replies.

"So, you don't drink and smoke at all. What do you do then?" Donna asked Jay.

Jay, happy to explain, "As of right now, just school, and sometimes I do live stream, and I do plan on making content online too."

"Oh, cool, what do you live stream? How many followers do you have?" she asked.

"I stream games, like first person shooters, and sometimes open-world RPGs." he said.

Donna explains, "I play games too, but only sometimes. My mom and dad love to play games too, so they introduced me to it."

"Oh, nice. That's interesting. What do you play?" Jay asks.

"First-person shooters and a bit of open-world RPGs too." Donna says.

"Alright, nice." Jay smiles.

"Do you plan on making a living as a streamer and content creator?" Donna inquires.

Jay responds, unsure, "Honestly, I'm not sure yet. We'll see how things go. If things go well, then I'll make it official, but for now, it's just for fun."

Donna is intrigued by Jay's life and future. She has a bit of fondness for him, though nothing too serious. The bus continues to roll on as they approach their destination.

"So, what about you Donna? What do you do? Or plan to do?" Jay asked.

She explains, though not entirely sure, "Umm... I don't know yet. Life is moving pretty fast, and we're already seniors in high school. We're almost 18, on the brink of adulthood, and I really don't know. But since you brought up streaming, I think that sounds pretty cool. I might give it a try. After all, I am somewhat popular, so maybe I'll give it a shot someday."

"Okay, that's pretty cool. If you ever need help setting up, come to me, and I'll hook you up with the best and get you started." Jay laughs.

"Ha! Yeah, that be nice." Donna lets out a laugh. As they talked the time flew by quickly. They made it to the state fair, and it was a bit packed.

It was afternoon, and everyone was having a great time. Jay and Donna remained close throughout the entire event, and the connection between them was remarkable. They appeared as a powerhouse couple. As time passed, they decided to grab a bite and some drinks. Jay treated her to the food they enjoyed, showcasing his generosity, and Donna found herself slowly falling for Jay.

She thanked him, "Thanks Jay next time I'll pay for you."

"Yeah, anytime." Jay smiled.

Jay has really liked Donna since Junior year, but she doesn't know that. He knows that she's single, but not sure of it as they never hangout like this before or had any actual time alone. He wants to ask if she's available to him but isn't sure if now's a good time. He's thinking maybe towards the end of the day he'll ask her if she's available for him.

Senior prom is months away. He knows that it's too soon to ask her for senior prom, but he doesn't wanna lose a chance with this girl. To play it safe and be secure he needs to save this for both of them tonight. That is his plan. As they walked to loosen up their full bellies in the carnival fair, time passed, and evening came.

"Hey Donna, are you single?" Jay asked.

"Why?" as she answers with a question.

He explains, "Well, because if you're single, and available then let's go to the senior prom together. I know it's early, but I don't wanna chance it, and later you end up with someone else. You know?"

"Yeah, but let me think about it for a bit. So, ask me again later or let's hangout some more."

"Yeah, we can do that. Can I get your number then?" he asked.

"Yeah." she smiled.

They exchanged numbers and it's evening in the summer and the sun is setting down.

Donna immediately starts texting one of her friends as they are soon almost done with the day.

They head out to the entrance of the fair standing on the sidewalk ready to be picked up.

"Do you have a ride?" Jay asked.

"Yeah, my best friend is picking me up? And I think you know her, It's Freya." she replies.

"Oh yeah, I know her, she's my friend too. Why is she picking you up?" he asked Donna.

Donna smiles, "Where gonna go to a party. Wanna come with us?"

Jay politely declines, "Sorry my ride is about to be here any minute now and I don't smoke or drink too so... but that explains why Freya didn't come to the fair with us."

Jay continues, "Hey so what's your answer-" but is quickly interrupted by Donna.

"Oh, Freya is here! Hey Freya, come here! Please take a picture of us."

"Alright." Freya said.

Donna tells Freya, "Here use my phone. I wanna get a group picture of all of us."

As the moment unfolded, everyone and all their friends who were at the fair stood ready to capture this moment. However, soon after, the crowd dispersed. Jay never had the chance to ask Donna about her confirmation for the prom; she left in a hurry but hugged and kissed Jay on the cheeks nearing his lips. Jay is surprised with how close that kiss was on his lips but soon felt a bit let down by Donna as she seemingly neglected his invitation.

His father picked him up, and they headed back home. During the ride, all Jay could think about was Donna. He wanted to send her a text, but he didn't want to be rude by interrupting her at the party. Jay finally arrived back home, where he lived with his parents.

At home Jay decided to text Donna about the prom invitation he made to her. He was eager to know her answer, but she didn't reply. He calls but no answer too.

Jay showers as he waits for Donna's reply, but still nothing from her. He's worried and calls Freya and she picks up.

"Hey Jay, what's up?" Freya answered.

"Hey, I called, and I texted Donna, but she didn't answer me back. What's going on? She's with you right?"

"Oh, she left with some guy and then I left afterwards." she explains.

"What do you mean? Is she okay?" he asked.

Freya explains, "Yeah, she's fine. She texted me like 20 minutes ago. Why? You worried?"

"Um yeah, I am. But why would she leave with a guy?" Jay asked.

Freya further explains, "I'm not too sure but she was making out with him and after that she told me she's gonna leave with him and so she did."

Hearing this broke Jay's heart as he really likes Donna.

"Oh, okay then. Thanks. I'm gonna go now." as he ends his call with Freya.

With the news that reached Jay, deep concern and a profound sense of despair engulfed him. He felt as though he had already lost her. His heart was breaking, and it seemed as if his world had come to an end. Agony coursed through him, and his body felt weighed down by stress.

The next day arrived, and Jay went to school, anxiously scanning the campus for any sign of Donna, but she was nowhere to be found.

Even in their shared class, her absence was conspicuous. During lunchtime, Jay sought out Freya to gather some answers.

"Hey so what's going on with Donna? I haven't seen her at all." Jay asked Freya.

"Ugh, her dumbass decided to just drop out of school. I don't know why. And I'm thinking it has to do with that guy she made out with last night." she explained.

Jay looks sad and confused, "How do you know this?" he asked.

Freya responds, "She told me over the text messages."

"Hold on. Let me see." as Jay looks at Freya's phone and sees the text messages.

Jay is even more heartbroken with such news. Him and Freya don't know why Donna would do such a thing. Donna didn't give many details and they're all left wondering in the dark.

Freya, "Hey Jay, I tried as soon as she texted me. I called her right away, but she didn't say much. I couldn't stop her, I'm sorry." she explained.

Jay walks over to a bench near the football field, consumed by his longing for Donna. Sitting there, he reflects deeply and is left in a state of uncertainty. A sense of weakness and darkness envelops him, as if his life is slowly slipping away.

Just then, his phone rings, and he sees that it's his mom calling. Jay picks up and answers the call.

"Hey mom. What's up?" Jay asked.

Judy, "Your dad wants to speak to you in person. It's urgent. So, I'm gonna pick you up right away."

"Okay then." Jay sadly responds without questioning.

In the car with his mom Judy.

"What's so important?" he asked.

"Your dad is gonna go into surgery very soon and so he needs to speak to you right away before he goes. Just in case he doesn't make it." Judy tells him.

Jay concerningly asked, "What? Why? Surgery for what?"

She cries and explains, "This morning your dad had a bit of a heart attack. I had to take him to the hospital. They said that he needs to do an open-heart surgery soon or it will get worse. But his chances of survival for the surgery is low. So, your father wanted to talk to you because this could be his last time here with us."

As they arrive at the hospital, Jay gets to catch up with his father before doing surgery the next day.

"Hey, how you holding up?" Jay asked his father.

His father, "Honestly I don't know. I guess we'll find out later. Anyway I called you here because this might be my last moment here. So I have a few things I need to tell you."

"Yeah." Jay replied.

His father said, "Jay, if I don't make it, I just wanna let you know that if it comes down to it, you're gonna have to be the man of the house. I know you're young but you're gonna have to be strong for me, your mother, and yourself. When people die it can be uhh….. very emotional and it can lead to depression and mental illness. I know your mother will not take it well if it goes down that way. So I need you to take care of your mother if gone."

"Yeah." Jay agreed.

His father continues, "It won't be easy if it goes down that route but whatever happens don't give up. Whatever happens try to take care of your mom and try to focus on yourself too when you can and do something good with life. Make something for yourself because you're almost an adult now. Stay strong and I love you."

On the inside Jay is emotional but he remains calm and strong. He held his head high and hoped for the best. He doesn't know what to really say but to only listen and agree with everything his father said.

Jay understands what his father is coming from and from this moment it only makes him stronger and matured.

During this period of Jay's life, it was very difficult. His father didn't make it and he lost a girl who he really liked and cared for.

When his father passed away, he slowly forgets Donna, day by day. Jay and his mother, Judy, now only have each other. Jay is now the man of the house and devotes to care for his mom with all he could.

Jay took a break from school for a whole month as he and his mother had fallen into depression and mourned for his father. He barely eats during this period of his life, but deeply cares for his mom.

Everything felt meaningless to him, but he remembers he's now the man of the house. When Jay and his mother went into depression, he had no choice but to thug it out for now. He puts all his care and love into taking care of his mom as she is not in a good mental state. She barely eats and constantly stays in bed.

Through losing his father, and going into depression, to taking care of his ill mother full time, Jay has completely forgotten about Donna.

When prom came by, he didn't go. He didn't realize that it came and passed by. It didn't exist to him.

During his last four months of high school Jay missed out on a lot on his education by streaming frequently throughout the week. Before turning 18 into an adult, he had already made $100,000 in his checking account.

His fan base during this time was over 100,000 subscribers.

When graduation came, he graduated with a 1.5 gpa and didn't give a fuck about his education as he is already winning and slowly living the life.

As soon as he got his high school diploma, he instantly left the school with his mom. Jay did no farewell and said no goodbyes, he is out with his mom treating her to a five-star restaurant.

In just two years of streaming and being a content creator, Jay had made significant progress. He moved out to live on his own in a luxurious house that is a bit further deep on the West Coast of California. In addition to his content creation journey, he joined an Esports team, which took him to various destinations for competitions and vacations.

His growth was swift and steady. By the midpoint of his second year, numerous brands and companies began sponsoring Jay.

On his third year he became a multi-millionaire and made new friends. He travels more but mainly for business and ESports. Within the third year of his career, he slowly began helping people here and there. He knows he can't help everyone but does the best he can to help.

Jay does give away for content, livestream, and behind the scenes. Along the way he ended up on the local news and globally. He is trending. He is a trendsetter. A lot of women are slowly hitting him up on dm. It makes him happy to see a lot of people filled with joy. At times his mom and friends tell him that he can be too generous. Thousands of people idolize him.

To some folks and younglings, he is seen as a hero to them.

On his fourth year he's already running two businesses. A clothing line and a very popular drink that's sold globally. Jay was making more than $5,000,000 a year. Throughout his fourth year he is met with a lot of women who only wants him for clout and money.

Some came close to getting dates with Jay, but they ended up ghosting him or the other way around where he is the one ghosting them. His luck with women hasn't always been very bright.

On his fifth year, in the present, before meeting Donna after five years. His current goal was to continue doing what he loves, but at the same time going out, and meeting more women to find the one.

He is open and ready, but a lot of women isn't worthy. His goal is to find and be with someone who can make him warm and be loved before the year ends. During this time, he joined some dating apps.

From here is where he met Donna for the first time in five years. He didn't know that it was her at first until now.

While taking a steamy morning shower, Jay reflects on all these moments from his life. He opens his eyes, completes his shower, and gets dressed. Heading out for a fast-food breakfast, he tries to eat, but his mind is overwhelmed, making it difficult to have an appetite. In the midst of his thoughts, he remembers Freya, an old friend of his and Donna's, and decides to reach out to her through social media, knowing that she follows him.

Jay is a bit nervous as he messages Freya. They haven't spoken since their senior year in high school, and he's eager to catch up with her.

Jay wrote and sent, "Hey Freya this is me, Jay. It's been a long time but how are you? Are you still in town? If so, wanna meetup and catch up?"

Momentarily she replies, "Oh hey it's been a long time. How's it going? And yeah, I am in town at the moment. I just got back but I'm only staying in town for a while so we should definitely catch up before I go."

"Alright let's meet up for some coffee. Can I get your number?"

"Yeah" she replied.

As they exchange contact, Jay gives her the location for them to meet up. It's a fancy coffee shop with vintage style. Freya made it to the coffee shop first, and Jay arrived soon after.

"Hey! How's it going Jay?" Freya asked.

"Pretty good." Jay smiled.

"So, what you been up to?" She asked.

"Just living life and live streaming and make content for my channel and I run two business." he replied

"That's nice." she complimented.

Jay politely asked, "Can I get you anything? What would you like?"

Freya smiles, "I'll get a large Caramel Frappuccino with extra whip cream on the bottom."

Jay, "Alright I'll get the same too."

Jay goes and takes the order for them and returns to sit down across from Freya at the same table.

"So, what about you? What have you been up to all these years?" Jay asked Freya.

She happily explains, "Well I was in school, and I just got done last summer. I'm currently working as a personal English teacher for foreign students. It pays really well, but I might change my career later so we'll see."

"Alright, nice." Jay compliments Freya.

As they talked the waitress came by and dropped off their drinks onto their table.

Waitress smiles, "Here you go, I got two large Caramel Frappuccino, with extra whip cream, on the bottom".

Jay and Freya both thank the waitress, "Thank you."

"Hey, do you remember Donna?" he asked Freya.

Freya's surprised, "Yeah, she was my best friend. What's up?"

"Do you keep in touch with her?" he asked.

"No, but the last time I did it was like what two years ago and she called me to ask for money that's it. And before that it was high school senior year since me and her keep in touch. That girl never calls or text me back until she asked for money." Freya explained.

Jay asked, "Do you know what happened to her? Or about two days ago of what happened?"

Freya confusingly says, "Ummm, no, I don't know what you mean. Why?"

Jay explains, "I met with Donna two days ago from a dating app. At first, I didn't recognize her. We went on a date together and after that she lured me into a trap with her boyfriend as they tried to rob me, and I ended up killing her boyfriend."

"No way!" she shouts.

"I'm telling you the truth. It's even on the news too." he explains.

Freya is shocked, "Well, what are you doing here then? Especially being in public talking about this to me. What happened to Donna? Did you call the cops on them?"

"No, I didn't. Why, you might ask, well, because she needs help, and I wanted to help her, so she ended up in the hospital to be cared for at the moment." he explained.

Freya is irritated, "Ugh, this is so stupid. I don't need to know anymore or anything about this. I moved on and I don't care about her. Let me guess you brought me here to feel sorry for her... or help her right? Is that it?"

"No, not really. At the hospital she didn't really give me much details or explain much, and she didn't want to talk to me much so that's why I wanna know exactly what happened to her through these years. But turns out you and her didn't stay in touch, so I guess that's that. And I didn't feel like asking her mom because I don't know her like that and so now, I came to you, to see if you know anything." Jay explains.

Freya sighs, "Well, if you really wanna know all I can tell you is what her mother told me when I was trying to stay in touch with Donna."

"Okay." he said.

She goes on to explain, "She was abused by her boyfriend. Physically and verbally. He threatens to kill her and her mom if she doesn't follow his orders etc. She does almost everything he told her to do. When her and her boyfriend needed money, Donna came to me and her mom asking for money. I helped her twice, but I already knew that I couldn't keep doing it as it was just wrong. And as you know Donna left home and school, she thought she found the one, which is just someone she met at a party, which she fell victim to. She's a dumbass and he wouldn't let her go see her family when she wanted to. She was constantly in and out of home with that guy. When her father died, he didn't let her go to his funeral, he told her to quit her job, and be with him 24/7. He goes on telling her she can always get another job and a whole lot of stupid shit. Me and her mom really tried to help, but it didn't work out."

"Damn, anyways, will you watch or be there when me and her stand trial?" Jay asked Freya.

She answers with an attitude, "No, why would I? Like I said I moved on and I don't want anything to do with Donna. This is all on you and her. And I'm only here for vacation so no, why would I be there for her trial? The fuck?"

Jay agrees with Freya, "Yeah, you're right I can see where you're coming from. So dumb of me to bring you here. I'm sorry."

Freya happily speaks, "No, no worries. I'm glad we caught up a bit. I'm happy to see. You're a nice man and some people see you as their hero. It was nice catching up a bit. Thanks for the drink even though I didn't drink it. I'm gonna go now."

Jay apologizes, "Yeah sorry for ruining the mood. You take care."

Jay gained some insight into Donna's past after catching up with Freya. He sat in the coffee shop, lost in thought as he gazed out the window. After a few minutes, he left the cafe and headed to his car. Jay pulled out his phone and began searching for a local attorney.

Upon searching, he found one of his interests and goes in for a meet and greet. There he is assigned, and they go over everything. Jay feels hopeful for himself but not too much for Donna. He is told to stay away from Donna and her mom and cannot speak of his case to anybody. All is set and ready to go as he heads back home.

In his house he sits there in the living room just thinking about everything that has happened.

In his mind, "What should I really do? What can I do? Can I even trust someone like Donna and her mom? Maybe my mom is right. Donna doesn't deserve to be helped. I should maybe testify against her. That way she can get more years behind bars."

Ding! Dong! His doorbell rings. Jay checks his security camera on his phone, he looks through the camera and he sees that it's the cop.

He goes to greet them, but he is met with a warrant by the cops for his arrest. Jay doesn't resist and doesn't say much as he already knew that this was gonna happen sooner or later. Jay is now arrested and is taken by the cops for interrogation.

At the police station inside the integration room Jay is met with two detectives. They pushed questions onto him, but he answered with ease and honesty.

He explains everything but of course there's no real hard evidence of Jay killing Terry in self-defense. The only evidence they found was surveillance security camera that showed Donna and Jay together out in public with Terry stalking Jay from a distance. After the integration Jay goes and pays for his bail and is released to go back home.

A week passed and Donna has fully recovered. She has left the hospital and heads over to where she will be reliving with her mother.

She knows she is soon to be integrated by the detectives. Her mother got her a lawyer and bailed her out until the court hearing. She knows what to say and do as they go over everything. She is told to stay away from Jay and speak to no one of their case.

Making it back home, Donna gets emotional as she hasn't been home much in the past five years.
She goes and lays down in her bed that she hasn't slept on for a long time. While laying down she cries and feels almost like a child just being there. She recalls how warm and sweet it was that her mother would tuck her in bed as a kid. Minutes later she goes into thinking about everything that has happened as she lays down just

staring at the ceiling. She closes her eyes and see's Jay in her mind.

In her thoughts, "Should I testify against Jay? Should I plead guilty? Should I prove Jay's innocence or frame him with what I could? I don't know. I feel so guilty, and I feel like I can't live with this guilt. Should I just kill myself? I know I will be behind bars for sure and I deserve it, but I feel like that's not enough for all the mistakes and poor decisions that I've made. I think I know what I must really do. I'm sorry mom... dad... and everyone. I'm sorry Jay. I....."

Deep in her thoughts, exhausted, Donna fell asleep.

Two weeks have gone by, it is now officially summer, and both Jay and Donna stand trial in the courtroom, facing the judge.

Outside of the courtroom building in public, the crowd is wild. Paparazzis, news reporters, and Jay's loyal fans have all arrived outside to witness this case.

Jay's loyal fans are there to support him all the way. His fans brought big signs to be flash in public to show their support. It's written, "We love you Jay. We believe in you." Another sign says, "We stand with you Jay." His fans shout and cheer for him.

Meanwhile some are booing and throwing backlash at Donna. They call her out and shout, "Whore!" to her. Some say in public to lock her up and have her pay for her crimes.

Outside in public of the courtroom building a news reporter interviews one of Jay's fans. The news reporter asked, "So, why do you support Jay? And who do you think is guilty?"

Jay's fan replied, "Well on the news they showed the surveillance security camera of the big breast girl's boyfriend stalking him. Not just that too but there is other footage showing her and her boyfriend where they robbed other people too and they were on the run for a while. So definitely this woman is the guilty one and from the looks of it, if i am correct they tried to set Jay up but failed miserably. And uh now we're here."

On social media most content creators are talking about Jay's situation. He is the headline of most news. The whole situation has a very big effect on Jay's reputation. Through it all Jay remains calm and strong and focused. Jay still hasn't made any public statement to his fans or friends. He must wait until the end of trial before making a public statement.

In the courtroom, Jay confesses to his killing out of self defense. He explains that he was scared and didn't know what would happen, and so he had to react quickly because for him it was a life or death situation. He reveals his beating and his threats that he made to Donna. He stands tall and confident with his confession.

The Judge asks, "Why didn't you call the cops, right away on Donna, in the first place after killing Terry? Why did you hold her hostage? What was your motive?"

Jay, with a strong presence, "Your honor, like I said, I didn't call the cops in the first place because I was in a life or death situation. I didn't wanna get robbed or be killed afterwards because that could've been the outcome after, if they had robbed me, and so I just had to react quickly. It had to do with my instincts and reflexes. Another part was I let my anger, my feelings, and vengeance took over me. I was deceived, I felt bitter,

I thought I was gonna get laid, but instead I was met with a gun pointed at my head. I never thought something like that would ever happen. From there on I was scared, angry, and so I beat her up and held her hostage. I threatened her to scare her, a bit of it was I did wanna have my way with her, but after a few minutes I snapped out of it. I know my thoughts were dark, to bitterness, violent, and sexual but i didn't rape her. That's not who I am, I've never said or done anything like that ever until that day of me being set up by Donna and her boyfriend. Like I said, I let my anger and vengeance took over. I am sorry about the threats I made to her. It was way out of line. I should've called the cops in the first place."

After Jay's confession the Judge has Donna explaining her side of the story..

Donna explains, "Yes your honor, everything Jay said is the truth. Me and my ex Terry who was my boyfriend at the time we planned to rob Jay and run away afterwards. Terry suggested that me and him was to run away, maybe Mexico after robbing Jay. It was arrogant and foolish of me and I will take full responsibility for all the crimes I've committed. And for the beating that Jay made to me I deserved it. I've committed some crimes and hurt my mother and my father. I can't forgive myself, I guess in a way I see it as if Jay was there to punish me for all my wrong doings, but at the same time setting me free from a dysfunctional relationship."

With power, The Judge, questions her more, "Besides robbery and theft what other crimes have you and Terry committed?"

She goes on to explain, "I shot a man on his arm. A week before the incident with Jay, my boyfriend at the time Terry, and I held up a jewelry shop owner at gunpoint. I didn't have the gun on me at first. It was Terry who had the gun, but he got into a physical fight with the store owner and dropped his gun. From there Terry told me to pick up the gun and fire at him and so I did. I didn't kill him but I shot him and wounded him. After that me and Terry took off with nothing in our possession. I didn't wanna do it but during that time I was scared of Terry so I ended up doing what he told me."

"Now about your relationship with Terry, what was it like? Why did you follow his orders? Why didn't you get help or break up with him?" The Judge asked.

With guilt written all over her face, Donna shamefully confesses, "My relationship with Terry was a very toxic, unhealthy relationship. There were many moments of physical abuse to verbal abuse, death threats to me, and my mom. He blackmailed me and my mom. I did what he said because I was in love with him at the time and he threatened to kill my mother constantly and I didn't know what to do. My mother did get the cops to get involved but they failed to help out. For that it gave me no hope at all from the authorities. And with constant threats being put onto me, I have to be by his side due to his possessive nature. He would tell me that if I am not by his side or if I break up with him, he will kill my mom in front of me, he told me he will kill me and then kill himself afterwards. I also didn't want to have my mom in danger and so I just went with what Terry's words. I was weak, I was naive, and I allowed myself to be manipulated. For that I am sorry"

"Now, Terry's family? What can you tell me? And where are they?" The Judge asked.

She said softly, "Your honor, about his family, I'm not too sure, I- I never met them, but he claimed to have killed his parents when I was with him. He told me he's the only child in his family, he told me he grew up nice and all, but one day after an argument with his parents he ended up killing his parents. That's what he told me and I wouldn't know where to begin because Terry never showed me where he used to live with his parents. Me and him were always living in motels and sometimes rented apartments. That's all he said and he never specified on how he killed them but he claimed to have killed them. It's possible that he did do it with how abusive he was to me."

Jay, hearing Donna's confession makes him feel sorry and sad for her. He is disturbed, but doesn't pity her. It's out of kindness and care that he has for her to the degree that it hurts him hearing such news. Dina sitting behind her daughter Donna, is in tears hearing all her confession. Jay and Dina remain strong.

The Judge continues to question Donna, "Now what crimes did Terry commit when you weren't with him? Is he affiliated with any gang members? Does he sell drugs? Does he use drugs? If so, what kind?"

She answers, "Yes your honor, sometimes he would do drugs. Sometimes he does cocaine and other times meth. Sometimes he would sell drugs too. He would sometimes sell the drugs that he has such as cocaine, meth, to marajuana."

"How about you? Do you do drugs? Or sell any when you were with him?" The Judge asked.

Donna with confidence, "No your honor. I don't do drugs and I don't sell drugs. He wouldn't allow me to get near it. But I used to do marajuana back then. That's it."

It's been over four hours and the case is at its final. All evidence has been brought forward and shown. Jay pleads not guilty and in the final court hearing he isn't found guilty and is let go free. Jay is innocent and feels a surge of joy and happiness taking over him. He is relieved. Jay happily smiles, but waits to hear Donna's side as it isn't over yet. Jay is eager to know what her fate would be in this final court hearing.

Donna pleads guilty to all her crimes as she wants to take accountability. In the final hearing in the court the Judge has made the decision.

The final results are in.

The Judge rules loudly, the verdict: "Donna, who has endured manipulation and abuse by her abusive ex. She will serve 30 days in community service and 30 days of mandatory therapy."

Jay and Dina are relieved. Happiness surges through them but they remain calm. Jay and Dina hold in their tears of happiness on the inside overjoyed but Donna and everyone in the courtroom is confused.

During the whole trial of their case Jay and Donna never mentioned that they knew each other back then.

Donna knows that she is guilty but is briefly paralyzed with confusion about her sentence. She froze and felt very odd. She is speechless and doesn't know what to say.

Donna's lawyer speaks, " Wha-what? Wow, that was easy!" as her lawyer turns to look at her. They're both just so confused.

As the Judge stands and ready to head out, Donna shouts, "Hey! What is going on? Why am I not serving jail time? Why are you giving me such an easy sentence?"

The Judge ignores her and walks out.

Donna continues to shout, "Hey! Wait! What's going on? Why? I'm so confused. This doesn't make any sense."

Her lawyer responded, "Hey, whatever it is, just take it as it is. This is good."

Donna stares down with no words left to say.

Dina happily and swiftly bursts into tears as she hugs her daughter Donna. They both hugged each other in the courtroom but Donna is not feeling it. Donna is getting mixed feelings about this whole thing.

Donna in a weary state, "Mom, I don't get it. What is going on? What happened? I'm guilty, I know I am. So why did the Judge go so easily on me?"

Her mom, in tears of joy, "It doesn't matter. I finally have you back and that's all that matters."

Jay's mother Judy, who is in the back on Jay's corner is furious with the outcome. She too is confused on why there is no real punishment towards Donna's crimes. She deeply stares at Donna with a dark look and dark presence in the courtroom. She then turns her eyes locked on Dina and then Jay.

Judy walks out of the courtroom with her overly bearing dark presence. Confused and lost in her thoughts, a dark hatred stirs and brews inside her. She feels a dark fire and darkness brewing inside her.

The case is now over and everyone heads out.

Jay is filled with so much happiness and joy as he heads home. He is glad that all this is over. The weight of it all has faded away.

When he reached home he was met with his mother standing at his front door. Jay stops and looks at his mother as she gives him a dark look with an overbearing dark presence.

Jay greets his mom, "Hey, Mom what are you doing here? Is everything okay? Why does it seem like you're giving such a negative energy?"

She smiles, "Yeah everything's fine, why? I can't be here to see my son after his win?" her smile darkens.

He smiles back, "Did you want to celebrate or something? You know there's no need to celebrate over something like this?"

"Why not?" she asked with a bit of sarcasm in her voice.

Jay continues to smile, "Well there's just no need too? You know?"

Judy with a very dark smile, "Oh, come on. Let's celebrate! Are you gonna invite me in? Or are you just gonna leave your mom out here?"

"Fine, let's pop a bottle or something." he happily gives in.

They head into Jay's kitchen.

Jay politely takes his mother in, grabs two glasses of cup for them with a bottle of wine. In the kitchen Jay, being a gentleman, fills up his mother's glass first. Soon after he fills in his glass and cheers with his mom as they both take a sip.

After the sip they both set their glasses on a kitchen counter.

Judy looks at her son with a dark presence.

"You seem different." she stated.

"What do you mean?" he asked.

"I don't know, you seem different, like you're more, happier than ever." she replied.

He questions her, "Okay, that's a good thing though right? So, why are you giving me such a weird and bad vibe?"

"How am I giving you a bad vibe?" she sarcasticly questioned.

"Mom? You, uh drunk already?" Jay asked.

Judy with a weary smirky dark look and smile, "No i can drink a lot. Pour me another one?"

Jay sighs, "Alright what's this about? Your glass is still half way full so I'm not gonna pour you one."

His phone in his pocket suddenly rings and he takes a look at it then puts it back in his pocket.

Judy, five feet across from Jay stares and tries to see who called.

Jay happily offers, "Wanna eat anything? I'm hungry, I can cook for both of us."

She ignores him. As he looks at his mom she is just zoned out with a dark presence. Judy is leaning against the kitchen counter holding the glass of wine in her hand. She's deep in her thoughts and stares into space.

It's quiet and Jay goes on to start prepping food to cook. His mom, still there just standing still with her deep thoughts.

It's quiet and peaceful for Jay. He feels very happy just prepping for food as he thinks about Donna.

He looks forward to seeing her.

Judy continues to sip on the glass of wine.

Jay, on the other side in his kitchen, facing his mom as he is prepping food. "I'm gonna make spaghetti, do you want some?"

A glass suddenly flew over in a blur and hit the wall near Jay. Sharp broken glasses everywhere next to Jay within three feet on his right side.

He immediately stops prepping food.

He quickly looks at the broken glasses and then glances over to his mom quickly. Her glass of wine is no longer in her hands.

They both stared at each sharpley. Jay gives his mom a serious look while his mom gives her a dark presence.

No words spoken. Just silence in the air in the moment with both of them locked eyes on each other.

Judy, she is just standing there, seven feet in front of Jay with such an overwhelming dark presence. She breathes in and out heavily.

"You need to leave now!" Jay shouted.

She continues to just stare, she slowly nods her head no left and right with her eyes locked on to him.

"I said leave now! Get the fuck out of here!" he shouted again.

He continues to confront her, "Why are you being like this?... You know what I don't need to know. Just go now!"

Hatred, angry, jealousy, and darkness erupts inside her. She breaks and she breaks out.

Judy in a dark toned voice, "You must think you're so fucking smart! Don't you? You must think I'm so stupid!..... If you think that i am stupid to not know what you fucking did. you! are! so! fucking! dead! wrong! I know exactly what you did."

"I haven't done shit. So, what are you trying to accuse me of?" he seriously asked.

"So, you wanna play dumb huh? You seriously think that I don't know what you did! What you did was scummy!" Judy shouts.

"I have no fucking clue what you're trying to say or get at. Can you please!!! Be more specific?" Jay shouting out loudly.

She sighs then turns her back on him and leaves.

Judy suspects her son Jay of something. She knows that Jay did something wrong. For that reason she is furious and angry with her son.

Evening closes in and night time arrives.

At the house of Donna and her mother they're both about to have dinner. Dina is cooking Donna's favorite meal that she hasn't had in a long time.

At the kitchen table, Donna sits and waits for her meal. She is still shocked and confused with everything that's happened at the courtroom. She was sure that she was supposed to be locked up and serve some jail time especially with all the evidence presented at the courtroom.

Donna's mom Dina is cooking across from her in the kitchen. She stares, looking at her mom just deep in her thoughts. Happy to be home, happy to be free, happy to be by her mother's side but guilt weighs heavy on her.

"Hey mom?" Donna calls out.

"Yes?" Dina replied.

Donna explains, "I just don't get it. How is this even possible? Is the Judge really that dumb? I was so easily let go."

Dina is happy and smiles, "Stop pondering on this. It's over and I'm happy that you're home and that is a blessing, so take it as it is."

"I don't know. It wasn't properly justified." Donna said.

Dina kindly explains, "Look, you've been gone so long, take it easy and relax. Don't let this chance go to waste."

Donna, able to piece something together in her mind and she suspected something.

She sighs, "Mom, what did you do?"

"What? What do you mean?" Dina asked.

Donna, so overwhelmed, "Nothing. Nevermind."

"Okay." her mother responded.

Meanwhile on the news shit is blowing up. Jay and Donna are trending. They are one of the headlines on the news. From content creators, streamers, and news anchors, are all talking about their case. Their case was very controversial. Donna was easily let go of her crimes and this really stirred up a lot of people especially Jay's fans.

Back at Jay where he lives, after the fight with his mother, and after dinner, he goes to take a warm steamy shower, after such a long day. With the case being over and Donna being set free Jay is filled with so much happiness and joy.

While relaxing in his steamy warm shower, he fantasizes about Donna. He's very curious about how she would look like being naked. His thoughts are very sexual. His sexual energy for her is very strong, powerful, and sensual.

In his mind he tries to picture her how she would look like being naked. He wonders what the color of her nipples are, how tight her vagina would be, to how gorgeous her vagina would look like. He leans towards pink for her nipples and areola because of her light skin.

He sees her large round breast with her nipples out in his mind vaguely, her curves, and her enormous butt sticking out.

Jay has an erection.

He continues to fantasize about her. He wants to have sex with Donna, his sexual thinking leads him to think of having a steamy hot shower sex with her. Jay's erection is very intense and very stiff.

He sees himself having sex with Donna in the hot steamy shower. He wants to hold her and carry her, while her big long legs, and her arms are wrapped around him, her big large round breast to rest on his chest, with her big wide butt mounted on his crotch as he thrust her in vagina in the hot shower.

He sees himself switching sex positions where he is standing behind Donna as she is facing the wall with her legs spread, her hands on top of his hands as he fondles her large breast with her back arched as he thrust her from behind into her vagina.

After showering he dries himself up with a towel and blows dry his hair.

He gets ready for bed and lays down to get comfortable, but only to find himself fantasizing more and more of Donna, while in bed.

With sexual thoughts, coursing through his body and mind Jay is very aroused. His erection and his thoughts further him more with wild imagination. He pictures Donna on top of him while laying in bed on his back. He sees and feels Donna's large breast resting on his chest while she rides him hard with her legs spread. He imagines how soft, heavy, and warm it would be to have her heavy figure just all weighing down on him with his arms around her body.

He fantasizes her in a new position, turning her over with him being on top of her, her large long legs wrapped around his waist, her arms around his neck, and her toes pointing down. Jay sexually sees himself thrusting her hard in the missionary position. Fantasizing himself in this position he wants to cum inside her and fill her up.

Jay fantasizes hard on Donna but doesn't masturbate. He doesn't play with himself. It's not Jay's style to touch himself sexually. He would rather have Donna touch him. Jay truly desires her and he looks forward to connecting with her.

He fantasizes Donna for an hour long, only to fall asleep soon after.

A new day arrives, in the morning Jay wakes up and he washes up. Jay finally made a public statement online on his social media. He made a 12 minute long video explaining his situation.

In the video he uploaded Jay stated everything but he doesn't mention knowing Donna from back then.

His fans are pleased to see him return but they are bitter towards Donna.

In the comment section of his video one fan said, "OMG! Jay is back. We love you man!"

A second fan commented, "Your case is a bit wild, what's so odd about it was that the girl wasn't given any proper punishment. Anyways, I'm just so glad that you're back."

Another fan commented, "It's so good to see you back. I'm so happy for your win."

His video was trending number one on the platform where he uploads. Within five hours he had five million views, 200k comments, and 400k likes on his video. It was a lot and Jay even gained 100k subscribers.

Jay has now reached five million subscribers.

He is thrilled to be back but his main focus is Donna. Though Jay is in a good mood, his mother Judy wasn't. She couldn't get any proper rest. When she woke up she instantly felt nothing but anger and hate. Her thoughts are dark and she feels like hurting someone or something.

During her morning she got up and washed up. After freshening up herself she made herself a very bitter black coffee and drank. She barely ate anything and headed straight to her company where she is the boss. While driving to her destination she did a lot of thinking.

A thought of a private investigator enters her mind. During this morning her mom decides to look for a private investigator. She pulls over and searches through her phone for one. She stumbles across one of her interests, she calls and get's a appointment right away to meet up in just a few minutes.

In just 20 minutes Judy arrives at the office of a private investigator. She plans on doing something. She wants to get to the bottom of something. Judy needs eyes and ears to look out for something.

In the private investigator office the private detective greets Judy.

"Hey there, how can I help you?" the private detective asked.

To Be Continued...

What do you think will happen next between Jay and Donna? What is Judy planning? What will happen?

You won't wanna miss it.

Hey there, this is Hanzo. If you're reading this and made it this far I just wanna say thanks for reading my first book. I hope you enjoyed this first part of the story as more is to come. I have planned to make this a two or three-part book series. I hope this drama, love story, and romance keeps you invested to see the next part that is on their way. It's only gonna get more interesting from here on out for Jay and Donna. I already have the story set on my end. I got the idea for this book through my personal experiences in life such as using dating apps and talking to women that never ended up well for me.

While I was on the dating app in autumn 2023, I thought a lot about women, dating, relationships, life and struggles. As I think more about it, I remember the time in early 2023, when I was in the car with my sister, listening to the radio, hearing about a man who got robbed by a woman and her boyfriend.

Some guy met this girl on a dating app where he thought he was gonna get to hookup with her when they met up but turns out it was a setup. The girl already has a boyfriend and they ended up robbing the guy at the meetup. I never looked into it to see who it was or if the culprits got caught or to see if it was on the news, but this gave me a lot of help for writing this story into a book. This is something that's very real and it can happen to you or me.

You might be wondering, what else made me decide to write this book or to just write a book at all in the first place. For me I've been struggling a lot in life, and I always have a lot of interesting stories in my head to tell.

During late summer of 2023 that's when it slowly started coming to me that I should utilize these stories and personal experiences into a book.

I wasn't doing well in life, and I needed to do something good and so I went with this.

I know that this book isn't big and the reason for that is because I'm new to all this and this is my first book. My English speaking and writing are also not the best. When I wrote this story, I had a lot of errors and I'm pretty sure you might've encountered some while reading this book. I had to edit my own writing and I did the best I could.

I don't know too much about the law and court system too and so for that I did not put much focus on the court case part of the story. Even if I let it go on into more details that will just make the story boring. My vocabulary and my grammar are not too good either. Once my life gets better, I will hire an editor to help me edit my writing.

Thanks for reading and thanks for your support.

Made in the USA
Las Vegas, NV
03 February 2025